Christmas Stories from the Heart

25 stories to rekindle your Christmas flame

Dr. Steve Jirgal

Published by The Core Media Group, Inc., P.O. Box 2037, Indian Trail, NC 28079.

Printed in the United States of America.

TABLE OF CONTENTS

DECEMBER 1
The Gift | 05

DECEMBER 2
A Time of Giving | 07

DECEMBER 3
The Birth of the Stars | 09

DECEMBER 4
The Birds of Christmas | 11

DECEMBER 5
The Christmas Star | 13

DECEMBER 6
Room In the Inn | 15

DECEMBER 7
Special Shepherds | 17

DECEMBER 8
After All, It's Christmas! | 19

DECEMBER 9
Christmas Friends | 21

DECEMBER 10
Finding Value | 23

DECEMBER 11
A Special Christmas Gift | 25

DECEMBER 12
The Blessedness of Giving | 27

DECEMBER 13
Christmas Disappointment | 29

DECEMBER 14
Lights for the Night | 31

DECEMBER 15
Special Words | 33

DECEMBER 16
The Tree by the Side of the Road | 35

DECEMBER 17
Joy Confirmed | 37

DECEMBER 18
A Donkey's Christmas | 41

DECEMBER 19
The Shine of Christmas | 45

DECEMBER 20
A Message from the Womb | 47

DECEMBER 21
The Song of Zacharias | 49

DECEMBER 22
The Gift | 51

DECEMBER 23
The Missing Pieces | 55

DECEMBER 24
The Seeds of Kindness | 57

DECEMBER 25
The Visit | 59

THE GIFT

"Thud" went the wreath on the front door. In frustration, Natalie got up from her chair, marked her place in her book and headed for the door to put the wreath back in place for what seemed like the twentieth time. She pressed the plastic hanger against the glass hoping that this time it would stay. She closed the door, leaned against it and gave a heavy sigh.

Christmas was a half-a-week away and her son was half-a-world away for another Christmas. He was serving in the U.S. Marine Corp. and he was all she had since her husband Harold has died four years ago. She loved Marty in a way that only mothers could understand.

Her mind flashed with images of Christmas past when he would come bouncing down the steps barely touching a tread. She could almost hear him squeal as he opened his stocking and presents. Natalie loved to cook, and Marty loved to eat. She smiled slightly as the scene of his plate overflowing with food flooded her memory. Marty had called from his post a week ago. He told her that he had been wounded in the leg but was alright. It wasn't life threatening but required a few stiches and a full round of anti-biotics. That was just enough to drive the dangers of war deep into Natalie's soul. "Another Christmas alone" she thought as she shook her head. Natalie was determined to make the best of it. She filled her lonely moments with reading, listening to music, and cooking for friends.

The timer in the kitchen broke her dreamy thoughts so she made her way back to the oven. As she donned her oven mitten and opened the door, she heard the familiar "thump" of the wreath falling yet again. Frustration filled her mind. She dropped the pan of cookies on the counter and threw her mitten on the table as she stepped toward the living room. She decided to bring the wreath inside and forget the idea of hanging it.

As she entered the living room, there she found the uniform outline of her son holding the fallen wreath. In three strides she was across the room and embracing the son she loved so much.

He dropped his cane and held her close and tight. He smiled and said, "Merry Christmas Mamma!" She wanted to return the greeting, but her voice was blocked by her heart. This was a new Christmas memory Natalie would never ever forget.

A TIME OF GIVING

The Milwaukee winter was living up to its reputation. Henry zipped his coat a little higher and shook his head at the car that once again wouldn't start. Luckily, it was only a mile to his house, and he could use the building on his left as a shelter from the wind.

He was equally lucky that he remembered to bring the gloves that his aunt had sent him on his birthday two weeks ago. Even with the delay he would get home in plenty of time to help with the decorations before their guests arrived. He loved the Christmas season, but he hated the hustle and bustle, the distractions, and frustrations it brought with it. "It's a time of giving" he heard himself say so many times frustrated at the selfish attitudes the season ushered in.

As he turned the corner, he was met with a blast of wind that chilled his face and numbed his ears. Amid the wind, he heard a voice very softly say, "Give him yours." He almost turned around to look for someone but knew he was alone. "What?" he whispered. "Give him yours" the voice in the wind repeated. Henry was confused and pressed on into the wind. Then it all made sense. Up ahead he saw the outline of what seemed like a pile of garbage by the curb. But Henry knew better. He knew that under everything was a man or woman seeking warmth over a sidewalk grate. Their collectibles and blanket made a home sheltering them from the cold. The voice in the wind did not speak again. It didn't have to. Henry knew when the voice of God was directing him.

As he approached the makeshift home, his pace slackened. He peered around a piece of cardboard to see a sleeping man covered with a blanket. Removing his gloves, he knelt, and placed them at the knees of the man curled up before him. Henry gave a heavy sigh and quietly breathed, "Merry Christmas."

Turning back into the wind, he stuffed his hands inside his pockets and with a faint smile on his lips, he whispered, "It's a time of giving."

THE BIRTH OF THE STARS

Many years ago, there were only three stars in the entire night sky. Three stars you ask? How can that be? But oh, my friends, these were not ordinary stars. These were stars of the highest magnitude. Their Blaze was sufficient to light up the whole canopy of darkness. And each night they dutifully took their places spaced away from one another so as to light up the darkened universe to the full.

Late one day as the sun began to go to its resting place, they waited in obeyance for the call of the angel directing them to their posts. But this evening was different. Instead of the angel turning them loose to glow in front of the deep backdrop, they were summoned to the presence of the Creator Himself.

He explained to them that this night was different and unique. He told them that He Himself would be going to the earth in the form of His son and that His life on earth would lead to the salvation of all mankind. This event He had planned since the beginning of time and would allow every person the opportunity to live eternally in the very presence of God. The Lord explained that although two of the stars would take their place, one of them, the largest would settle over the very dwelling of the Messiah. The Almighty commanded that the largest star would carry this duty. The stars were dismissed with two of them taking her usual position and the largest one directed to Bethlehem.

The very large star dutifully took its place and begin to glow and glow and glow. As the importance of this evening continued to settle in on the star it found itself shining and glowing brighter than it ever had. "The Savior is born!" The Savior is born! Salvation has come! Mankind is saved! Peace on earth!" As these words continued to resonate deep in the center of the star, a strange vibration began to grow as well. It got stronger and stronger as the star burned brighter and brighter. Then as the star watched from the heavens it witnessed an unforgettable event. From behind a door three figures appeared. Immediately the star knew that these were the parents of the Messiah and the Christ child himself. And as the blaze of that star continued to grow, the mother of the child removed the covering from the babe's face. And when the star obtained a full look at the face of the Savior it was beyond its ability to control itself.

With unspeakable joy and excitement, the outward glow and the inward vibrations joined together and caused that giant star to burst into billions of stars each glowing with the same message "The Savior is born! The Savior is born! Salvation has come! Mankind is saved. Peace on earth!"

And yes, my friends the stars we see on the clearest of nights still glow and still vibrate and each one of them still shares that enduring message "The Savior is born! The Savior is born! Salvation has come! Mankind is saved! Peace on earth!"

THE BIRDS OF CHRISTMAS

Joseph helped Mary off their small donkey and held her arm as they slowly walked to the shelter. They were both surprised and disappointed that the small city was full of visitors leaving no rooms available for them. Still, they were thankful to find a place that was safe and out of the weather.

"I didn't think my baby would be born like this" Mary said as she worked her way to the side of the stall. "I'll be with you. You can do this," Joseph replied as he placed a blanket on the ground and guided Mary toward it.

Joseph put another blanket on top of his wife and began gathering sticks and straw to build a fire and warm their temporary home. When the first sparks ignited the straw, he added twigs and wood and soon had a nice little fire lighting up the corner of the room. As the flame began to grow, he heard Mary say, "Joseph, it's time." Joseph moved to Mary's side and held her hand. A few hours later the young mother gave birth to their first son whom they named Jesus.

But as the boy was being born, small brown birds began to appear at the front of the stall. First one, then another, and finally a total of ten birds all lined up close to the fire. They stood still watching the young girl labor and bring forth their son. And as they watched, they began to do two things: They started singing and slowly moving their wings. Their song brought comfort to mother and baby and the movement of their wings gently fanned the flames of the fire bringing warmth to the new family.

Because of the kindness in ministering to the Son of God, the Heavenly Father gave them a special and unique mark upon their bodies. The next time you see a Robin Red Breast:

> Remember the birth of our Savior on that special night.
> Remember the kindness of those small birds.
> Remember to send the warmth of a loving deed someone else's way.

THE CHRISTMAS STAR

Tom cupped his hands together and breathed hard into his palms as he fought against the cold and made his way toward home. It was Christmas Eve, but somehow it didn't feel like it. Christmas was a time when all the world should be perfect and at peace. But all Tom felt was confusion and emptiness.

At the office, they were supposed to get off work early, but his plans were interrupted as an "emergency" order came in. His wife had burnt his favorite Christmas cookies which Tom had looked forward to all day and even the carolers who stopped by their house every year didn't show.

And now he had to walk home from delivering gifts to friends across town because his old Buick had broken down again. He didn't even think to bring a heavy coat or gloves. The cold seemed to cut right through him as he hustled his way through the middle of town.

"This is a Christmas I could do without!" he thought as he leaned into an unforgiving wind. "Once, just once, I'd like to have all the missing pieces fit together like they're supposed to."

As he passed by the town's small park, he glanced at the manger scene. It was truly lovely. But something was missing. Tom stopped directly in front of the life-size figures.

“Unbelievable!” he fumed. “How could anybody forget?” How could they leave it out?” Tom hadn’t noticed it before, but this year there was no large blue star above the manger.

Without Tom’s notice, a small b oy had paused beside Tom to gaze at the manger scene. “Isn’t it pretty?” he said. “Everything looks so perfect!”

Tom couldn’t help himself. Before he knew it he blurted out, “but it isn’t perfect! Someone forgot the star! It just doesn’t seem like Christmas when the star is missing!”

The boy looked up and smiled. “They didn’t forget the star!” he said. And then he pointed his little mitten covered finger at the trough where baby Jesus lay and said, “He’s right there with Mary and Joseph!” With that, he turned and scurried down the street and into the darkness.

Tom stood as still as the figures before him. A smile broke out across his face as the truth of the little boy’s words echoed in his head. “Jesus is the star of Christmas” he whispered as he spun about and pressed toward home.

ROOM IN THE INN

Bart and Olivia were duly proud. They were listening to the leader of the rescue mission. She was telling them how thankful she was that their son Tom had given his car to the mission. This was not a surprise to the pair, for they knew that although Tom didn't have a big bank account, he always had a big heart.

They saw his open heart early in his life. They recalled with ease the night the three of them attended the Church's Christmas play. Little Tommy was about four-years-old and his eyes were transfixed on the stage.

On the way home he asked his parents why Mary and Joseph had to sleep in the barn. They reminded him of the scene where they were told there was no room in the inn. Tommy fell silent re-running the entire play in his mind.

At home, the family had a light snack and then it was time for Tommy to mount his bed. Burt and Olivia tucked him in and after praying with him, kissed him good-night.

But just as Burt wasa about to turn off the light, Tommy called for his attention. "Hey Dad" he said. "Yes son," Burt replied removing his hand from the light switch and stepping toward his son. With his head rising slightly from the pillow Tommy said, "If Mary and Joseph came to our house, they could sleep in my bed and I could sleep on the couch."

“God bless you son” was all that Burt could whisper. He smiled, turned out the light and closed the door. Olivia met him in the hallway with a hug and the two fought back tears of pride as they walked down the hall.

And so began the growth of a young boy’s generous heart—a heart that never stopped growing in its desire to give.

SPECIAL SHEPHERDS

Looked down upon by those around,
The young men led their sheep from town.

Up with the sun, on every day,
A job to do, they made their way.

They fed the lambs from fields each day,
Protecting them from every prey.

Their task the others would not do,
For with the sheep, it's never through.

And then one night with stars so clear,
The saw a sight so very near.

An angel from the Lord on high,
Appeared to them, and lit the sky.

Their hearts felt weak, their heads did spin,
When from his mouth, he spoke to them.

"Fear not!" he said in a voice so strong,
"The Savior is born, though time was long."

To a star he pointed to show the way.
"Go now" he said, "Before the day."

Then he was joined by a heavenly choir,
With praises to God going higher and higher.

The men left the sheep and ran to the town
Over hills and fields without slowing down.

'Til they finally arrived at the place of His birth,
And they knelt by His bed and felt such great worth.

To be told of this act while on the hill they did stay,
They looked at the child and had nothing to say.

For before them He lay, the child of the King,
The one that the prophets said time would soon bring.

So with a smile on their faces as broad as the land,
They all left there rejoicing with the message in hand.

Though the world looked down on those men of the sheep,
They all felt much larger with this story to keep.

For that night was the night, of which all people sing,
They saw a host of angels and knelt by the King.

AFTER ALL, IT'S CHRISTMAS!

It was the Christmas season, and tensions were mounting with the speed of the calendar. Brian and Nancy were almost done with their Christmas shopping and were enjoying a cup of coffee while seated next to the fireplace at the local sandwich shop.

With the coffee and conversation complete, they gathered themselves to leave. Nancy leaned into Brian and softly said, "Let's leave a big tip. After all, it's Christmas!" With reluctant agreement Brian pulled a five-dollar-bill from his wallet and laid it atop the seven-dollar check.

As they worked their way through heavy traffic, Brian struggled to maintain his patience. His frustration was evidenced by the grip with which he held the steering wheel. No one seemed to be driving with any common sense and all signs of courtesy were nowhere to be found. Nancy placed her hand gently on Brian's forearm and said, "Honey, it's okay. Try to relax. After all, it's Christmas!"

When they stopped to pick a few things up at the grocery store, they passed the Santa-clad man ringing the bell above the red metal bucket. On the way out, Nancy nodded toward the man while tapping Brian on the back. She followed her motions with a whisper, "After all, it's Christmas!" Brian rolled his eyes and dropped three singles in the hole in the center of the bucket.

Arriving home, they had to stop part way into the driveway because the trash can that had fallen over again. Brian gave a heavy sigh while shaking his head. He opened the door to exit the car and quickly rectify the situation. It was at that moment that he heard a load thud coming from the other side of the car. Walking around the vehicle, Brian quickly learned what had happened.

Danny Sinclair, a boy from two doors down, had slammed his bike into the door panel of their car. “I’m sorry Mr. Hanson! I didn’t mean it! I couldn’t stop. My brakes don’t work.” Looking down at the small dent the boy’s tire had made moved Brian’s voice into stern lecture mode. He was just about to turn his words loose when in his mind he heard Nancy say, “After all, it’s Christmas!”

So, with a calm voice, he simply said, “Try to be more careful son.” Then he watched as Danny rolled away on his bike with the front tire wobbling from a slight bend.

Later that evening, Brian announced that he had to go out for a few minutes. Without waiting to explain, he was out the door and backing the car out of the driveway.

Just before dinner, Nancy noticed Brian pull the car into the driveway. A smile leaped to her face as she watched her husband pull a brand-new bicycle from the trunk and wheel it up the sidewalk toward Danny’s house.

Moments later, Brian returned and before his hand could reach for the handle, Nancy opened the door and embraced her man. With a smile as big as the holiday, she heard him whisper, “After all, it’s Christmas!”

CHRISTMAS FRIENDS

John and Reggie loved people and bringing them together for a party was one of their favorite activities and this Christmas was no exception. The energy in their home increased with the coming day and everything was loosely planned for a great time. The list of invitees was over a page long and hopes were high that everyone would come.

When the evening arrived, the party was in full swing with each room on the main floor packed with people. Food and drinks were placed at various tables among the guests and the laughter, music, and smiles seemed endless.

After some time had passed, several couples had gathered and were seated in a back room catching up with long-time friends. During the conversation, a family's name was brought up followed by several comments. But one couple, Tom and Lisa looked puzzled. The asked about the family and confessed that they didn't know them. The others seemed surprised as the family was large and well known in the neighborhood. The couples continued in their confusion when suddenly the unthinkable was realized. They were at the wrong party! They asked about the present address and discovered that they were a block away from the place to which they were invited.

With sincere apologies to John and Reggie they sought their coats and quickly made their way to the front door. The hosts told them emphatically that they were welcome to stay but with chagrined faces they exited. When they left, those who were aware of the mistake chuckled at the miscue.

Moments later the doorbell rang. There on the steps stood the embarrassed couple. They decided to rejoin the party and asked permission to re-join the others. The door was swung wide and in no time, they were re-engaged in the joy of the evening noting several times that the party they were supposed to attend couldn't be any better than this one.

And on that evening during that Christmas party, a new couple was added to John and Reggie's list of friends.

FINDING VALUE

There was a small blanket,
The family tossed aside.
Other blankets took its place,
And also took its pride.

The days did pass away,
And frigid nights did come.
But the little blanket just laid there,
Not taken by anyone.

Then one night some strangers came,
A man with a soon-to-be mother.
And the blanket was tossed to her,
To be used on way or another.

And the blanket then wrapped a child,
And in it the dear one curled.
And it held that baby close,
And found its worth in the world.
Just a little used up old blanket,

No use for anything.
But that time worn tiny blanket,
Once gave warmth to the King!

And just like that little blanket,
The world would pass you by,
Not much for them to think about,
They leave with just a sigh.

You might feel you're nothing special,
No reason to garner pride.
But your heart will be rejoicing,
When the King is found inside.

A SPECIAL CHRISTMAS GIFT

It was as cold as it was dark, and as usual, Mark was running late. He had been delayed at the office and at this point the Christmas party would be well under way. He had called his girlfriend Laura twice assuring her he would be there and that he was on his way. Both calls brought mini lectures on responsibility and the importance of getting to the party.

About two miles from the party site, he was working his way through traffic when he passed a car stopped by the side of the road. With a quick glance he noticed an older couple seated in the front seat. A thought of pity flew through his mind, and he re-focused his attention on moving ahead. But just as fast as the sympathetic thought left, it came racing back. Without debate, Mark swung his car into the nearest parking lot and seconds later was approaching the disabled vehicle.

As he walked toward the car, he could see the flat tire in the rear. When he got closer, the window slid down and he learned the extent of their dilemma. Henry and Alice were on their way to the hospital to visit their son when their tire blew out. Alice had left her phone at home and the battery on Henry's had died so they had no way to call for help. The folded walker in the back seat further showed the extent of their problem.

Mark offered to change the tire understanding that this delay made him even later for the party. He knew Laura would not be happy, but he determined that he had no choice but to help the older couple.

But when he opened the trunk, he found another problem. The tire wrench was missing. He thought he could remedy that by using his own but quickly learned it was the wrong size. The only option was to drive the struggling couple to the hospital himself. The hospital was twelve miles away in the wrong direction and he was certain he was in for another lecture, but he dialed Laura's number anyway.

His misgivings became reality when Laura told him that he should have called someone else to help and he should be with her at the party. He tried his best to appease her, but it didn't seem to help.

On the way to the hospital, Mark learned that Henry and Alice Johnson had been married for over 55 years and were traveling to visit their only son Hank who had been in the hospital for over a week. He was battling cancer and the outlook was dim. Conversation continued the entire way to the hospital and Mark was enjoying getting to know the elderly couple.

When they arrived at the hospital, Mark pulled up to the main door and helped Henry and Alice out. He learned then that Alice was the one needing the walker. He walked them to the lobby and told them he would be back in after parking the car. Having parked the car, he walked quickly through the hospital door with the goal of getting the Johnsons to their son's room.

The three of them walked slowly to the elevator and road to the sixth floor. The Johnsons invited Mark in but he declined sharing with them that he was late enough for the Christmas party. He wished them well and headed down to the main lobby.

While working his way back to the car, Mark replayed in his mind the conversations he had with Laura. He knew at this point that she would be beside herself with anger and he didn't look forward to the uneasiness of the encounter. As he left the parking lot and waited at the light, his mind began to focus on the possible conversations they would have with him telling her that he had no choice. These were people who needed help and their struggle eclipsed his need to go to a party. He was sure that Laura would counter his argument and he was equally sure she would be angry for a couple of days.

It was with these thoughts that he changed the left blinker to a right one and turned to head home. His dominating thought became, "Maybe my friends are right. Maybe, just maybe, she's not the girl for me anyway."

THE BLESSEDNESS OF GIVING

Lee walked out of Kenny's room shaking his head while emitting a heavy sigh. "He wants all five action figures" he complained to his wife Kathryn. He dropped down on the couch and continued his frustration. "They're not cheap and we don't have the money. Why can't he be satisfied with one? We'll let him pick his favorite. But he told me repeatedly that it just wouldn't be a good Christmas unless he had all five."

Lee shared with Kathryn that he felt that Kenny, their seven-year-old son was being selfish and that he was going to miss the real meaning of Christmas because of his attitude. Kathryn agreed but passed it off as normal for young children to only think of themselves.

Lee went to bed that night with worries holding his mind hostage. With the recent cutbacks at work, he knew that this Christmas would be a lean one. With a heavy heart he finally fell into a fitful sleep.

The same scenario followed the next night with Kenny insisting on getting all five actions figures. Lee tried to talk him out of it hoping to instill a heart of gratitude for any gift, but Kenny continued in his persistence with tears.

And with Christmas two days away, Lee felt his discouragement climbing. There was no money in the bank and bills had piled up. Work had slowed down even more giving another dent to his slim income.

But that night the phone brought a glimpse of relief. The caller agreed to buy eight books that Lee was desperate to sell. The books had been in the family for years and held a tinge of sentiment. But they did nothing but take up space on the shelves of their tiny home. So, parting with them only made sense.

With the transaction completed, Lee made his way to the store. He had enough to reluctantly buy all five action figures with a little left over for a small gift for Kathryn. He purchased the toys and asked for a couple of extra paper bags to be used to wrap the gifts.

Kenny would have his desire met and his parents hoped it would bring some level of happiness if only temporary. If only his boy could understand that Christmas is not about getting what you want. It's about love, and joy, and peace. It's about the birth of the Christ-child—God's greatest gift to the world. Lee pondered these thoughts as he walked through the chilly streets toward home.

Christmas Eve arrived and their little home was filled with laughter and music. Soon Kenny sauntered to bed sharing his hope regarding his desire for the five action figures. After Lee settled into his room, he met Kathryn at the kitchen table where they both worked on wrapping the action figures and putting together some small gifts in a sock that served as a stocking. In the stocking they placed an apple, an orange, a few pencils, two pens, some chewing gum, and three small pieces of chocolate. These items served to fill the makeshift sock completely.

A short time later, Kathryn stepped into Kenny's room and found him in a deep and peaceful sleep. When she left the room, Lee noticed a smile on her face, a piece of paper in her hand, and a tear fighting to leave her eye.

She walked over to her husband, gave him a hug, and handed him the paper. Lee looked at it and saw scrawled on the page Kenny's name and the names of his four closest friends. Next to each name was the title of each of the action figures he requested. In a flash Lee understood what Kathryn had already concluded. Perhaps their son did have a good idea of the meaning of Christmas after all.

CHRISTMAS DISAPPOINTMENT

It was a few days before Christmas and ten-year-old Jacob was sitting on the porch eating a snack. As he finished, a group of older boys came riding past. He always enjoyed it when the older kids came by and waved him into joining them. He could be on his bike and down the street in a flash. And that Saturday morning was no exception.

Jacob saw the four boys coming and after they called to him, he yelled his intentions to his mom and grabbed his bike that was leaning against the side of the house. Moments later the five of them headed down Banner Street and turned to go down Jefferson Avenue.

They stopped for traffic and saw Mr. Crenshaw walking away from them. Mr. Crenshaw was a seventy-three-year-old man who lived at the end of the block. His wife had died seven years before and he lived alone and kept pretty much to himself. Beyond that, few people knew very much about him. Several young people spread the usual rumors about him which no one made an effort to correct. It was said that he had been in prison for selling drugs or for killing a man. Others said that he was wanted by the police for robbing a bank. Word was even shared that he murdered his wife.

All this served as motivation for the boys to begin taunting him. As he made his way up the opposite side of the street, they yelled to him. One boy said, "Hey Crabshaw! You goin' to the store to buy a friend?"

Mr. Crenshaw heard the boy indicated by his slight turn toward them followed by a shaking of his head. Another one of the crew yelled, "You lose your hearing aid?" This was followed by one of them saying, "Nah, he's heading over to rob the bank." This he said to his companions, but it was said loud enough for Mr. Crenshaw to hear. After each comment the boys joined one another in laughter.

Getting no reaction from the old man, the boys turned in the other direction and peddled away looking for their next adventure. Although Jacob didn't do any of the hollering, he was very much a part of the verbal assault, demonstrated by the nodding of his head and his laughter. In a very strange way, the encounter made Jacob feel accepted and in a stranger way, he felt good inside even if it was at the expense of Mr. Crenshaw.

After covering a good bit of distance with the young men, Jacob wheeled his way toward home. His mother announced that she needed to go to the store to pick up a gift for Jacob's uncle. Uncle Jerry was coming through town, and she wanted to make sure she had a gift for him. Jacob volunteered to go with her and before long they were parking the car and walking toward the store.

Not long after getting out of the car, they heard the familiar sound of the bell being rung by a man clad in a Santa suit. When they got closer to the door, Jacob quietly said, "Hey mom, got any change?" His mother smiled while opening her purse and dug out a few coins. She handed them to Jacob, and he slid away from her and stepped toward the red bucket.

Jacob dropped the coins in the kettle while noting that the money would be used for the local rescue mission. As the coins fell into their new home Jacob's face fell on that of the bell ringer. It was Mr. Crenshaw! The revelation startled Jacob and he almost revealed his surprise by stepping back. He thought about apologizing for the earlier encounter but realized that Mr. Crenshaw never saw him. With that in mind, he rejoined his mother and headed quietly into the store.

For several Christmas seasons after that Jacob reflected on that one. He always noted that there were several Christmas mornings that he was mildly disappointed in the gifts he received. But that was the very first Christmas that he was truly disappointed in himself. And from that day on he never encountered Mr. Crenshaw without showing him the respect worthy of the elderly.

LIGHTS FOR THE NIGHT

The small rural town of Layona had a wonderful tradition. Each Christmas the huge tree in the center square was decorated with an amazing number of lights. And on the large tree, the people of Layona were welcomed to place whatever ornament they chose. The tree remained unlit until the night before Christmas. Then on Christmas Eve, everyone gathered just after dark for the lighting of the massive tree. The center of town was literally swarming with people of all ages as friends and family gathered. It was an incredible time of music, dancing, singing, and laughing and everyone looked forward to that special night. The joy of the evening was culminated in the mayor shouting "Merry Christmas" to the massive crowd followed by the flipping of the switch. When the tree was lit the faces of those gathered was lit as well and the great cheer could be heard for miles.

But one Christmas Eve, the town leaders found they had a very big problem. When they tested the lights that morning, they learned that they would not come on. They tried the circuit breakers, the electrical connections, and the main power source. They even changed all the electrical cords joining the lights to the main outlet and replaced the switch. Nothing seemed to work.

They each felt a deep sense of frustration matched by their disappointment. Putting their heads together, they decided to carry on with the festival that evening as planned. All the other activities would take place, but the lighting of the tree would not.

Word spread quickly in Layona and the disappointment spread just as fast. How could they really celebrate without the lighting of the tree? It just wouldn't be the same! The faces of young and old alike displayed their feelings and a slight heaviness was felt throughout the town.

Nonetheless, the people gathered, and the square was packed. There was the usual music and dancing and a good bit of laughter, but everyone knew the big event would be tainted with the lack of the lighting of the tree. It seemed that the evening would simply end when those gathered just wandered back to their homes.

But that night something special was destined to happen. An angel of the Lord was about to visit them and turn their disappointment into the highest of celebrations and a night no one in Layona would forget. Amid all the music and celebration, a peal of thunder was heard. This was followed by a small light that could be seen in the distance. The light got brighter and bigger as it approached and in moments the music and conversation stopped, and all eyes were locked on the sky. Some thought it was a plane while other believed it was a meteor. But no one doubted that it was a move of God when the massive light swept over the crowd and blasted past the unlit tree.

The light was gone as quickly as it came but the effect remained. The tree which was supposed to serve as a climax to the evening was now lit and it seemed to be brighter than ever before. For several moments the crowd stood silently until someone shouted, "Merry Christmas!" With that the entire mass of people cheered and shouted, "Merry Christmas!" at the top of their lungs.

The tree remained lit for the rest of the evening then finally faded out as the last person headed home. But what never faded from the hearts and minds of the people of Layona was the night that an angel visited them and blessed them with the greatest Christmas celebration ever. The memory of that night still comes blazing back to their memory whenever anyone shouts, "Merry Christmas!"

SPECIAL WORDS

Kenny and Michelle sat in the pew remarkably and understandably proud. Their daughter Ellie was singing a featured solo in the youth Christmas play at their church. Ellie had an unusually strong and clear voice especially for a twelve-year-old and all those present clearly enjoyed her special talent.

But things were not always so celebratory for the family. For some unexplained reason, Ellie spent her early years in silence. Multiple tests had been run and she was found to be in sound health. None of the medical experts had any answers for her inability to verbally communicate.

There were no outbursts of anger and no squeals of delight. Ellie was simply a content little girl who never expressed herself in words. She frowned when she was displeased and offered a slight grin when overjoyed. Each of her four birthday celebrations saw her demonstrate her approval but never to the point of words.

Ellie's parents continued to provide for her and endeavored to find answers from the medical community. But the answers never came. The experts were as puzzled as Kenny and Michelle and simply couldn't find the reason for her silence.

Then when Ellie was almost five years old, the family ventured out to enjoy the Christmas

Eve service at the church. The presentation was well done, and everyone present enjoyed themselves.

On the way home they noticed a "Live Nativity" at a church not far from their own. They decided to swing by and spend a few moments at the sight. The presentation was very well done. Of course it included Mary, Joseph, and Jesus. A donkey and lamb were present as were three wise men, and two shepherds.

The family stood there enjoying the scene when Mary adjusted the baby from one arm to the other. As she did so, the blanket covering the baby shifted as well and the entire face of the baby came into full view.

Then the remarkable happened. Just as the baby's face became uncovered little Ellie smiled, raised her arm, and pointed. Then she exclaimed loudly and clearly, "Baby Jesus!" And in that very moment, the dam of her silence was broken and her expressions were released to her voice culminating in the wonderful gift of singing that has brought joy to all the hearts of young and old.

THE TREE BY THE SIDE OF THE ROAD

The seed fell from the sower's bag
And landed on the ground.
The other seeds stayed with the man
And made it into town.

Alone and off the trail it grew,
But never quite so big.
It wasn't very much of a tree,
Not worth a man to dig.

Through hot day and cold nights
The tree never understood
The plan the Lord had for it,
His plan is always good.

As the seasons came and the seasons went,
The tree stayed by the road.

And folks would often stop by it,
To cool off from their load.

Then one special day two folks came by,
A man and his expecting'bride.
They stopped and paused beneath the leaves,
And from the sun did hide.

And after cooling off a bit,
The two rose up to leave.
But a few days later they returned,
But now the two were three.

And so that little tree did know,
Its purpose in this life.
To give relief to a man,
With a special son and wife.

JOY CONFIRMED

It was Christmas Eve and Jenny and Dean wove their way through the parking lot at the Senior Center. Jenny said, “I hope mom will like it. I know she doesn’t have one like this.” In her hand was a small gift wrapped in colorful Christmas paper.

Jenny was carrying a crystal figurine of a dancing ballerina. Over the years, her mother had collected these small figures and had gathered quite a few. Back home, she had a shelf displaying dozens of them and they were truly beautiful. She was so proud of them and was quick to share where she had discovered each individual piece of her treasure.

But a few months ago, she suffered from a stroke which left her deeply incapacitated. She never spoke and only moved with great help. Total care had to be given by the staff and most of the time she was found to be in a deep stare without visual response. It was clear that her condition was quickly declining.

Jenny and Dean came to visit her regularly. They would come in, greet her, and then share what was going on in their lives and around the world. Even though her mother gave no sign of knowing they were there, still they came and sat talking to her receiving no response. Each visit ended with a hug from Dean and a kiss on the cheek from Jenny. And each time they left with a sadness over her condition.

On this Christmas Eve Jenny had secretly hoped that the gift would spark some kind of reaction from this woman she loved dearly. She longed for some response showing them that she knew they were there. A faint smile, a nod, a squeezing of the hand would have made Jenny's heart leap with joy.

As they entered the room, they both cried out, "Merry Christmas Mom!" But their enthusiasm was only met with silence and her mother's blank stare. She was seated in an overstuffed chair facing the window with a banket on her lap. Jenny leaned over and delivered her usual kiss on the cheek. Then sitting on the bed, she extended the gift toward her and gently said, "Merry Christmas mom!" Her mother never moved. Jenny said, "We got you a special gift. We hope you'll like it!" Then Jenny placed the gift in her lap and unwrapped it. Holding the figure before her eyes, Jenny said, "Look mom, it's a ballerina!" I know you don't have one like this. Isn't it beautiful?" But her enthusiasm was only met with the usual stare from this formerly lovely lady. Jenny quietly placed the gift on the window sill in front of her.

Jenny and Dean talked to her for a while and then left after giving her their usual contacts and wishing her a Merry Christmas. Jenny fought the tears as they gently closed the door and silently walked back to the car.

In the car, Jenny said, "I wish I could be sure that she liked it. I wish I knew that she even understood that we were there." And then the tears came. Dean put his arm around her and held her as she wept. He had no words for her as no words were needed. After a few minutes, Jenny gathered her emotions and the two worked their way back home.

On Christmas day, Jenny and Dean celebrated together with a light breakfast and the traditional exchange of gifts. It was a happy albeit quiet time, and they were thankful for each other and the many years they had together. They each answered texts from their many friends and prepared to go over to the nursing home for another visit.

But their morning was interrupted by a call from the Senior center. Little information was given regarding her mom, but they were encouraged to come down to the center. Both Jenny and Dean knew that something had happened and suspected that her mom was no longer with them.

They quickly got prepared and within an hour were walking into her mom's room. There on the bed they found her lifeless mother. She looked so lovely and peaceful. There was no sign of discomfort or worry. She simply looked as if she was enjoying a peaceful rest. Both Jenny and Dean cried while understanding that her mother now was finally at peace and experiencing the joys of heaven. Although her mother was no longer there, through her tears Jenny talked softly to her. Then with Dean's hand on her back, she rose, kissed her mother's cheek, and whispered, "I love you mom!"

Dean embraced his wife and said, "It's all good now. She's with the Lord." As he continued to hold her, Jenny wiped the tears from her eyes, and while resting her head on his chest whispered, "I know. I know."

As they turned to leave, a nurse opened the door and stood to the side. "I'm so sorry!" she said. "Please let me know if there is anything I can do." "Thank you" Dean said as they began to exit the room.

"There is something that we thought was interesting" the nurse told them. Both Dean and Jenny slowly turned to face her. Walking over to the bedside, the nurse reached down and pulled part of the blanket away from Jenny's mom. Tears flowed freely from both Dean and Jenny when they saw her mom's hand. It was next to her heart and held the lovely crystal figurine.

Dean and Jenny both stared in silent amazement. Then Jenny broke the silence and said, "It is all good now!" and they left the room with a great sense of blessing.

A DONKEY'S CHRISTMAS

Jasper was an old donkey. In fact, he was older than his owner Elam who purchased him shortly after he and Rebeccah had married. Understandably, he had become part of the family and Elam, Rebeccah and their two children treated him as such.

Jasper was unusual in that he never seemed to fight against any of the demands placed on him as most donkeys do. Although he was old, he was still fairly strong though he struggled with arthritis in his left shoulder and both knees. This made rising at the beginning of each day difficult and very painful.

Still, he did whatever he was commanded to do without hesitation or braying. He pulled the cart to the market, carried loads of wheat and barley to the town center, and transported passengers to their desired destination. He even held still as the children played with him occasionally braiding both his mane and tail.

Jasper didn't understand the details but knew that something different was happening. Just before the family retired for the evening, Elam came out to the barn and led him to the feed bin and water trough. This he usually did to give Jasper extra strength when an upcoming chore was at hand.

In the morning Jasper was blanketed and led with his characteristic limp to a nearby home.

At the home, Elam and a young man named Joseph talked. "He's old but still strong" Elam said. "If you move slowly, he'll get you to Bethlehem. It would be best if you rode by cart but the wheel on the cart is damaged and cannot be fixed." Joseph shared a smile and thanked his uncle for his kindness. The trip was very long and there was no way Mary, his expectant wife could make the long trip on foot.

Moments later Mary exited the house and hugged the kind man. "Thank you," she said putting her hand on Jasper and stroking his neck. Then with little effort, Joseph lifted her onto Jasper's back and with a wave and a smile the two began their journey with Mary riding comfortably on the faithful donkey's back.

Jasper limped along with Joseph by his side. Every few miles they stopped to rest and each evening they were hosted by relatives along the way. After a week of traveling, they came to their destination, Bethlehem.

But this evening there were no relatives for them to join. They were escorted to a barn not far from the main house. A woman had given Mary two blankets and several pieces of cloth and apologetically bid them good night.

As Jasper looked on, Joseph constructed a make-shift bed and led his wife to the resting place. He gave Jasper some oats and water and while patting his neck quietly thanked him for his service.

In the middle of the night several candles were lit, and a great commotion was heard in the barn. Jasper didn't understand it but knew something important was happening. A woman from the main house was summoned and she was joined by two other women. Jasper was lying down, and Joseph sat next to him. The two of them watched and waited as the women helped Mary in her distress.

A short time later the cry of a baby was heard, and Joseph raced to his wife's side. The women left, and as the sun rose, Jasper could see the face of the baby boy.

Then something special and unexplainable happened. As the mother nursed her baby with Joseph sitting near, a gentle and warm wind swept through the barn. Then softly, very softly a single and distinct word was heard-"Rapha" (healed). Mary and Joseph were both surprised and confused by what had happened and shared a bewildered stare.

Then the answer came as they watched Jasper rise and approach them. Without words they both recognized that his noticeable limp was gone. There was no swelling about his knees and he stood before them strong and whole.

That was a special night for Jasper, for not only was he healed, but he heard the cry of a child and knew that he had not only carried a woman who was to have a baby, but the baby she had was the King.

THE SHINE OF CHRISTMAS

Tony was so excited as the Christmas lunch got started at the office. It had been a good year for the company and the bonus checks were anticipated to be a bit bigger than previous years.

On credit, Tony had spent his bonus in order to buy some extra gifts for his wife Molly and their two young children, Adam and Andrea. But the greater balance of credit was spent on himself-a brand new gold Rolex watch.

He knew a couple of the men at work who had them and they seemed to jump off their wrists when they extended their arms. In Tony's mind the watch said, "I am somebody!"

But after buying the watch, Tony was amazed at how quickly the emotional shine faded. The watch looked great and told time with complete accuracy. But beyond that it was surprising how little effect it had on him.

Christmas morning was equally disappointing. The gifts were opened in a frenzy and befoe long the kids were on their own to play with them. Molly was thankful for her gifts—a new outfit, a couple of books, and some jewelry. These too, were set aside as she nestled by the fire to leaf through her magazine.

Something had taken the spark out of the holiday for Tony and it didn't take him long to realize what it was. He quickly came to the conclusion that what was leaving him so empty could be summed up in one word—opportunity.

The local Outreach Center had sponsored a special drive to feed and clothe one hundred needy children that year. Outside their building they had erected a plywood sign with a vertical red band indicating their progress.

Tony passed the building each day on his way to and from work and he couldn't help noticing the movement of the red band. Each time he felt his heart pulling for them to reach their goal, but it never pulled hard enough to move his wallet from his hip in participation. After all, his gift plans would devour his bonus especially the one he had planned for himself.

And as Tony exhaled a heavy sigh, he inhaled a determination not to let that opportunity pass him by again.

The following Monday morning, he was late for work. He stopped by the store and returned the treasure that adorned his wrist. Then he made his way to the Reach-Out center in hopes of finding someone there.

Surprisingly, an elderly man was there taking care of a few things in the kitchen. Tony introduced himself and asked if it was too late to make a donation. The man shared his affirmation and moments later Tony was walking toward his car with the satisfaction that he had been part of the center exceeding their goal.

While driving home, he looked at his wrist several times. His watch was gone and his wrist was empty. But with equal clarity he knew that his joy was back and his heart was full.

A MESSAGE FROM THE WOMB

"I know what I know, and I know what I felt," said Elizabeth to her cousin Mary and the two older women seated in her home. "I have carried this child whom we will be calling John for six months and all has been quiet in my womb. In the last two months he has moved very little. Now and again, he seems to stretch and roll but does little else."

"In fact, there were three or four nights when I lay down that a fear would come over me. His lack of movement brought a deep fear upon me. I was afraid that my son was not well. I even had thoughts that I would lose him. But then as I remembered the promise of God—that I would have a son, a great peace would come over my heart and I would drift off to a deep sleep."

She nodded toward the window where her husband Zacharias could be seen seated under the awning. "While serving in the temple last year, Zacharias had a visit from an angel of the Lord. Though he has been unable to speak since that day, he has let me know that we are to have a son and his name is to be John."

All three ladies smiled and nodded as Elizabeth continued. "This boy will fulfill the vows of a Nazarite and he will be used by Jehovah to turn the hearts of the people back to God and to lead the way for the promised Messiah."

The smiles from the ladies continued as Elizabeth leaned forward grabbing Mary's hand and speaking with added emotion. "But Mary, when you entered our home just now and I heard your voice, this child within me leaped as I have not felt him move. This was not a stretching of the arms, or a roll of the body. He leaped as one does when overcome with joy." Elizabeth smiled broadly and wiped a small tear from her eye, and added, "My baby leaped and my voice cried out in praise of what the Lord is doing through the two of us."

The two older ladies each placed a hand over their hearts and gently nodded in wonder. Elizabeth continued, "The child within you has joined his heart with my very own and I know that your son will do great and mighty things. This is the day that I know Jehovah is fulfilling His promise and bringing His kingdom to earth."

All four women gave silent nods of agreement and pondered all that had taken place. They each donned the smile of wonder and satisfaction as their hearts and minds rejoiced. To see prophesies fulfilled is a wonderful thing. But to be at the center of that prophesy brings joy beyond words.

THE SONG OF ZACHARIAS

For temple work I set my feet,
To do the work of the Lord.
But found a message very rare,
Which no man can afford.

An angel came to me that day,
Bringing a word from God's hand.
A son would soon be born to us,
With a message for our land.

I thought it strange that this should be,
A child from my child-less bride.
I silently laughed and hid my face,
But my heart I could not hide.

He told me that she would have a son,
A boy that we'd call John.
And he would lead our people back,

To a life from where we'd gone.
He'd be a man to pave the way,
For sinners to come back.
And he would teach them how to gain,
The holiness they lack.

From sinful things he'd stay away,
And never take in wine.
His head of hair he'd never cut,
This holy son of mine.

The angel my voice, he took away,
In knowing of my doubt.
So hard for me to know these things,
And never bring a shout.

But then the day when family came,
I knew that it was true.
This boy would someday pave the way,
For Christ to come in view.

And when we traveled to God's house,
To bless him with the crowd.
They asked us what to call the boy,
"His name is John" I said out loud.

And now a son is born to Mary,
The Messiah and the King,
He'll save us all from our sins,
And God's blessing He will bring.

He'll preach and teach and lead us,
To holiness from above.
And through the way He lives His life,
We'll know the Father's love.

THE GIFT

The Christmas season was under way and so was Leslie's job as an aide at the Senior Retirement Center. The learning curve was high, but she seemed to be catching on fairly quickly. She was enjoying her time at the center helping with medications, meals, and activities. The residents seemed to like her as well and were quick to engage in a conversation and to invite her to play the many games they enjoyed in the recreation room.

An exceptionally large Christmas tree was placed in the dining room and Leslie noted how it was adorned with so many colorful lights and a host of various ornaments. She learned that many of the ornaments were made by the residents, and they were eager to share with Leslie which ones they had made.

Leslie also noticed a box on a table by the entrance to the room. Next to the box was a stack of cards with places for names. She wasn't sure what it was but noticed several people putting their names on the cards and dropping it in the box. Comments like, "Maybe this will be my year!" and "I hope they pick my card!" led her to believe that a big gift was in the works for the winner. The sign on the table said the drawing would be next week and her excitement grew with that of the residence.

Leslie found her mind wandering from time to time. It kept coming back to the tree and the big gift to be won. What could the present be? Perhaps a new T.V., special meal, or the latest recliner were to be given. She asked several workers as well as a few patients but only received vague answers. As the calendar moved, her curiosity rose.

Finally, the big day came. People were dressed well and seated at tables all around the dining room. A fine meal was being served and conversations and laughter were in abundance. The air was filled with excitement and celebration. Those living there as well as quite a few guests were present. A new ornament was placed at each seat to be hung on each person's small tree in their room. A local church led in several traditional Christmas carols, and everyone seemed to be having the time of their lives.

After the carols, dessert was served followed by the director getting up and giving a short speech along with reading the Christmas story. Then she directed everyone's attention to the box on the table. "Finally," Leslie thought, "this is going to be great!"

All eyes were locked on the director and the entire room fell into a deep silence. Some even seemed to be holding their breath. Reaching into the box, the director pulled out a card and read the name. "This year's winner is...Ms. Penny Fincher!" The room erupted with applause as Penny stood and gingerly worked her way to the front.

Leslie positioned herself to have a clear view of the front. She noticed that Penny's grin never faded and that she seemed like a local celebrity. There were smiles and nods and a few pats on the back as she walked toward the director.

Leslie's eyes scanned the room to see where the gift was but saw nothing. The director simply handed her a small box and Penny held it up before the cheering crowd. While she stood there, a small set of steps were rolled into the room and Penny turned to meet it as it stopped beside the tree.

At the base of the steps Penny held the box up while opening it to the delight of the crowd. The box contained a beautiful silver star that blazed in the lights from the tree. Finally, it was all coming together for Leslie. She watched as two workers helped Penny mount the steps using the railing both for support and lift.

A worker followed Penny up the steps and held her waist as she reached up to place the star on the top of the tree. With the star in place, Penny bowed to the crowd who responded with applause and a standing ovation from those who could rise.

At that moment, Leslie came to a clear understanding that sometimes the greatest gift is not what you get to have, but in what you get to do. And with that thought she smiled and nodded tucking away her insight for future reference.

THE MISSING PIECES

George loved jig-saw puzzles and usually assembled eight to ten large ones each year. In all likelihood, his appreciation for the activity came from his father who assembled them as well. His wife Rachel surmised that the puzzles reminded him of his father and his childhood and although putting them together never interested her, the finished product always did.

As the Christmas season started, George sat at the side table and broke out a new puzzle. It was an oversized puzzle revealing a beautiful nativity scene and naturally George thought it was appropriate.

George hoped that their four-year-old son Jimmy would enjoy helping him but found that his young mind could not stay fixed on the subject. Still, every time George sat at the table Jimmy climbed on his lap for a short time and enjoyed "helping" his father.

One evening, a couple of days before Christmas, George placed the last few pieces in place and announced its completion to the family. They gathered around the table marveling at the beauty of the picture.

The colors were vibrant and the details were captivating. The scene was complete with Mary, Joseph, the shepherds, wise men, two lambs, a camel, a brilliant star and of course,

Baby Jesus. There was a particular glow about the manger that immediately drew one's eyes to the child.

Jimmy had lots of questions and George and Rachel patiently answered each of them to the level his young mind could absorb. Every morning for several days Jimmy would gravitate to the table, climb up on a chair and be found staring at the picture.

Early one morning as George was about to leave for work, his eye casually scanned the puzzle. Immediately he noticed a problem. As he stepped closer, he discovered that several pieces from the center were missing. He brought it to Rachel's attention noting that Baby Jesus was not in place.

Without discussion they both headed down the hall to Jimmy's room. Jimmy had just awakened and was in the process of climbing out of bed. They said "Good morning" and asked about the puzzle. Without a word, Jimmy reached under his pillow pulling out several pieces and handing them to his Dad.

Jimmy smiled and without shame informed them "I didn't want Jesus to sleep alone." George bent down and scooped up his son as Rachel leaned over to kiss the young boy's cheek.

THE SEEDS OF KINDNESS

It had been a long journey and Joseph helped Mary off the donkey and guided her to a blanket placed in the shade of a tree. He poured a handful of oats and a small cup of water and put them before the donkey who devoured both immediately.

Then he joined his wife who lay on her back gently rubbing her enlarged belly. "It won't be long," she said as she sat up to drink from the cup in Joseph's hand. "I cannot wait for the promised one!" Mary nodded, turned toward him and took another swallow of water. "To see all that has been promised come true is a wonder that goes beyond my words." Joseph smiled and nodded as he wiped a bead of sweat from her brow with the edge of his gown. "My words cannot be found as well."

Moments later Joseph and Mary were approached by a small wagon carrying Benjamin and Sharone who were making their way from Bethlehem. They exchanged pleasantries and the strangers shared some of their water and an apple with Joseph and Mary. Looking down Sharone noticed the sweat on Mary's face. She pulled out a handkerchief and wiped Mary's face placing it in her lap. "Please keep it. You will have a use for it when the time comes." Mary grabbed the cloth, smiled, and nodded. After words of peace Benjamin and Sharone headed their way leaving Joseph and Mary to continue their trek to Bethlehem.

Joseph helped his bride to her feet and lifted her onto the donkey. But the effort caused the small piece of cloth to fall from Mary's hand and it was left behind as they moved away. Unmoved and untouched the handkerchief lay in the dirt. By and By, the dew of the morning and the dust of the day covered the small piece of cloth.

Then something strange began to happen to the decaying fabric. Small sprouts of life began springing in its place. Several days later several buds could be seen from the stems. And in short order, the buds burst open to become the most beautiful and colorful roses.

The plant continued to grow and spread to a few feet tall. The vibrant color of the rose was a light pink on its edge and a scarlet color at its core. The flower sprouted in place of the fabric and today it is known as the "Rose of Sharon," and its beauty can be enjoyed all over the world.

THE VISIT

Mary rubbed her forehead and followed that by placing her two hands on her abdomen. She stared at the ceiling and replayed in mind, the experience she had just had.

It had been a strange night, the strangest of her young life. As usual, she lay down in her small home attached to her parent's house. The day had been busy but no more than usual. But as she began to sleep into sleep, she felt a strange sense of peace come over her with that peace came an unspoken message that all would be well.

Just before dawn she was awakened by a soft but hollow "thump." Without alarm or fear her eyes remained closed as she wondered what it could be. Then she felt a warm vibration-like sensation in her belly. Again, she was without alarm but wondered what might be happening to her.

Gaining no outside prompting, Mary rolled over to her side and upon opening her eyes was greeted by a very bright light. She was captivated b its brightness yet at the same time wondered why it didn't hurt her eyes.

Mary sat up and stared directly into the light still mesmerized by what was taking place in her room. Then a voice both deep and clear gently spoke to her. She leaned further toward the light, and she was told, "Mary you are a blessed woman, and the Lord is with you. Do not be afraid. The Lord's favor rest on you. You will bear a son and you will call Him Jesus."

Mary's brow furrowed as she answered, "How is this to be since I am a virgin and have known no man?"

The voice continued, "Nothing is impossible with God. The Holy Spirit and the power of God will overshadow you."

Mary's breathing increased and through short gasps she said, "I am a servant of God. His will be done."

With that the light in the room faded and Mary was left alone to ponder all that had just happened. And as she lay there deep in thought a enduring peace flooded her soul followed by a smile showing both her contentment and amazement.

ABOUT THE AUTHOR

DR. STEVEN A. JIRGAL

Dr. Jirgal is a 1980 graduate of Gettysburg College where he became a four-time conference champion, All-American, and inductee to the Middle Atlantic Conferecnce *All Century Team* in the pole vault. He holds an undergraduate degree in health education and physical education. Following graduation, he taught on the high school and college level while coaching football and track in both venues. He holds masters degrees in health education, sports medicine, and divinity, as well as a doctorate in ministry.

He has been the director of Sports Medicine at Wingate University, area director for the Fellowship of Christian Athletes and has served on the staff of Hickory Grove Baptist Church in Charlotte, NC, as well as leading Lakeview Baptist Church, in Monroe, NC and Anderson Grove Baptist Church as the Senior Pastor. He presently serves as the "Pastor to the Pastors" at Lee Park Church. He has served on the local board of directors for the Fellowship of Christian Athletes, the board of trustees at New Orleans Baptist Seminary and the ministerial board of Wingate University. He currently serves on the board of directors for The Carolina Study Center, and Fathers in Touch ministry.

Dr. Jirgal is the founder and director of *The Jirgal Leadership Institute* where he strives to equip people for success in leadership roles. He and his wife Pam have three children, Joshua, Caleb, and Sarah. They reside in Monroe, NC.

OTHER BOOKS BY DR. JIRGAL

(DESCRIPTIONS TO BE FOUND ON THE JIRGAL LEADERSHIP WEBSITE AT JIRGALLEADERSHIP.COM)

The Path of a Champion
Dying to Live
Life Points
Laws to Live By
Principles of Wholeness
Running a Clean Race
Encounters with the Christ
The Going to Bed Book
Intentional Steps
52 Words
Mining the Mind of King Solomon
From the Pages of Qoheleth
Life in the Pearl

www.ingramcontent.com/pod-product-compliance
Lightning Source LLC
Chambersburg PA
CBHW080811020826
48982CB00017B/934

* 9 7 8 1 9 5 0 4 6 5 5 0 7 *